I Can Read series

The favourite children stories and fairy tales in the
I Can Read series are specially written for Early and
Beginner Readers. They are written to help young
children on their first step to independent reading.

All the titles in *I Can Read Level 1* series consist of
simple texts using approximately 200 easy and
commonly used words. The words are repeated often to
facilitate word recognition. The sentence structure is
kept simple to encourage children to read
independently. The colourful illustrations,
which match the text closely, will help children to
predict the story line. It will add further enjoyment
to the reading process.
For a pleasurable shared-reading experience, details
based on the illustrations could be added and discussed.

The titles in *I Can Read Level 2* series have longer texts.
Each story is around 300 words long. The structure of
the sentences is slightly more complex as it progresses
from the simple words and sentences of *Level 1*.
The illustrations continue to form an important part of
story-telling and are important tools to help a child
predict and read words and sentences. The titles in
Level 2 aim to encourage and further develop the habit
of independent reading among young children.

I can read
level 1

Jack and
The Beanstalk

There was a boy
named Jack.
He lived with his parents
on a farm.
They had a golden harp
and a magic hen
that laid golden eggs.

One day, a giant came by.
He stole the magic hen
and the golden harp.

Jack's parents
became very poor.
They had no money
to buy food.
They had to sell their cow.
On his way to the market
Jack met a stranger.

"Will you sell your cow," he asked,
"for three magic beans?"
Jack agreed.
He took the magic beans
and went home.

Jack's mother was angry.
She threw the beans
out of the house.
Next morning Jack woke up.
The magic beans
had grown
into a giant beanstalk!

Jack climbed up the beanstalk.
At the top,
he saw a strange land.
He came to a huge castle.
A lady giant opened the door.

The lady giant gave Jack
some food to eat.
Suddenly Jack heard
loud footsteps.
"Hide yourself," said the lady.
"It's my husband.
He likes to eat children."
Jack quickly hid
under the table.

It was the Giant!
He had the magic hen
and the harp.
The Giant had his lunch.
Then he fell asleep.

Jack grabbed the hen.
He jumped
out of the window
and ran home.

"Our magic hen
is back!"
his mother
cried.

Jack went back again
for the harp.
But the giant woke up!
Jack had to run very fast.

The giant took his heavy club.
He ran after Jack.
Jack climbed down
the beanstalk.
The giant followed.

Jack got down quickly.
He took an axe.
He chopped down the beanstalk.
The giant tumbled down.
He was dead!

"Well done, Jack,"
his mother cried.

Have you read
all these books
in Level 1?

Puss In Boots

The Hare and the Tortoise

Little Red Riding Hood

Peter and the Wolf

Beauty and the Beast

Jack and the Beanstalk